ANCIENT ADVENTURES

COUNTY DURHAM & NORTH YORKSHIRE

Edited By Lisa Adlam

Years of

First published in Great Britain in 2016 by:

YoungWriters

Coltsfoot Drive
Peterborough
PE2 9BF
Telephone: 01733 890066
Website: www.youngwriters.co.uk

FOREWORD

Welcome to 'Ancient Adventures - County Durham & North Yorkshire'.

This collection features stories from 7-11-year-old children who were given the challenge to write their own adventure inspired by past events. These mini sagas could be up to 100 words long.

It was clear to see that the pupils really got inspired by the competition.

I have had the pleasure of editing this anthology, and the entries published here show just how exciting history can be. They cover a wide range of topics from World War II to Queen Victoria, from dinosaur encounters to the eruption of Pompeii. The stories are by turns funny, dramatic and poignant.

All the entrants featured within should be proud of their achievement and I hope this experience of exploring the past will encourage them to continue writing in the future.

Lisa Adlam

CONTENTS

Alex Buckingham (7)	65	Caitlyn Stansfield (8)	105
Alfie Baker (8)	66	Daniel Phillipson (8)	106
Rehan Ashraf (8)	67	Lana Thomson (9)	107
Tanwyn Smith (8)	68	Ethan Sawyer (8)	108
Nathan Easby (9)	69	Oliver Stonehouse (8)	109
Poppy Ashley (10)	70	Isabel Caddick (10)	110
Dominic Hopton (8)	71	Zach Latcham (10)	111
Elliott Wright (9)	72	Isabella Kathryn Walton (8)	112
Amelia Coates (9)	73	Jack Atkinson (10)	113
Evie Thompson (7)	74	Ryan Lynch (9)	114
Ava McCulloch (8)	75	Poppy Tapster (7)	115
Elleanor Waddington (8)	76	Sam Parry (9)	116
Charlie Lythgoe (9)	77	Lilia Long (8)	117
Ben Mills (8)	78	Beth Ward (9)	118
Lily Allcock (10)	79		
Isabelle McQuade (9)	80		

Great Smeaton Academy Primary School, Northallerton

Emily Dixon (9)	81	Oliver Elsdon-Whitfield (10)	119
Emily Davidson (9)	82	George Gayer (10)	120
Benjamin Farrow (8)	83	Fran Marshall (9)	121
Max Edwards (9)	84	Bethany Brown (11)	122
Sam Patton (9)	85	Maegan Sharp (11)	123
Emma Nary (8)	86	Casey Chapman (11)	124
Lily Webster (8)	87		
Harry Robson (9)	88		

Green Gates Primary School, Redcar

Ryan Mills (8)	89	Kacey-Leigh Brunton (9)	125
Bonnie Bennett (8)	90	Jasmyne Walker (9)	126
James Morton (8)	91	Ruby Campbell (9)	127
Annabelle Staniford (8)	92		
Ava McSorley (8)	93		

Kader Academy, Middlesbrough

Jakub Powlowski (8)	94	Isobel Coe (9)	128
Isobel Vaughan (8)	95	Lucy Richardson (9)	129
Olivia Edwards (10)	96	Evelyn Woodward (8)	130
Katie Tuffnell (10)	97	Alexander Hasler (9)	131
Ashton Smith (9)	98	Harry Bell (9)	132
Emily Garbutt (11)	99	Zahra Rashad (8)	133
Grace Daniel (8)	100	Iqra Ali (9)	134
Kingsley McCarthy (8)	101		
Sarah Adamson (8)	102		
Alex Davison (10)	103		
Harriet Christie (10)	104		

Alisha Hussain (10)   135
Naiomi Pye (11)   136
Skye Chen (8)   137
Biba Lairini-Taylor (10)   138
Scarlett Armstrong (10)   139
Brandon Pollock (10)   140
Heidi Elizabeth Peat (9)   141
Kai Hodge (9)   142
Elizabeth Morrissey (10)   143
Goodness Onuh (8)   144

Levendale Primary School, Yarm

Hannah Armstrong (8)   145
William Carr (8)   146
Max Norman (8)   147
Ellis Leason (8)   148
Oliver Kibble (8)   149
Holly De Main (8)   150
Ruby Walton (8)   151
Amelie Rose Kibble (8)   152
Lucy Makepeace (8)   153
Lois Hudson-Foster (8)   154
Grace Forster (8)   155
Abi Edwards (7)   156

Silver Tree Primary School, Durham

Emily Leaver (8)   157
Harvey Johnson (8)   158
Charlie Martin (8)   159
Jack Wilson (8)   160
Ellie Snowdon (8)   161
Bailey Martyn (8)   162
Ryan Cleminson (8)   163
Lucy Sugden (8)   164
Ellie Ayre (7)   165
Tyler Rennie (8)   166

St Margaret Clitherow's Catholic Primary School, Middlesbrough

Isabel Dobson (11)   167
Christopher Brown (11)   168
Isabel Willet (11)   169
Leigh Davey (11)   170
Ben Wright (11)   171
Annie Williams (11)   172

THE
MINI SAGAS

Bernard's Burnt Beard

Bernard was a hairy Stone Age man because he didn't have any hairdressers like you and me. He didn't even have a razor because there was no metal invented. One morning, Bernard went out for a stroll and collected some sticks for a fire. When Bernard got back he made a fire but his beard caught on fire instead.

'Ahhh! Help!'

'Hmm? What was that?' wondered another hunter

'Oh, me, I'm a hunter named Bernard.'

'Looks like you've burnt your beard! Go and have a dip in the lake and I'll make you a house out of stone.'

'Thanks mate!'

Sophie Middlemiss (7)
Barley Fields Primary School, Ingleby Barwick

Encountering The Great Barrier Reef

'Land ho!' shouted the lookout from the crow's nest and all of a sudden there was a loud *smash,* followed by the sound of splintering wood.
'We are taking on water,' shouted Cook. 'All hands below deck.'
The crew were running around in the dark, trying to bail out the water.
'It's not working!' shouted Groves. 'We are going down.'
'We need to lighten the ship,' shouted Cook. 'Throw the guns overboard.'
Alas, the Endeavour was stuck on the Great Barrier Reef.

Megan Farley (8)
Barley Fields Primary School, Ingleby Barwick

The Corn Thief

On a dark night, suspiciously creeping through the farm was a poor man obviously up to no good. Suddenly, he sprung into action, stealing corn and a horse. Packing the corn into his bag, he swiftly made his escape on the horse.

Next morning, the farmer rushed to tell King Arthur about the stolen items.

'Find him!' bellowed the king.

The king's guards located the thief selling the corn in the market square. They chased him to a cliff edge where Merlin the sorcerer caught him in a magic bubble and took him to the castle where he was beheaded.

Thomas Swash (9)
Barley Fields Primary School, Ingleby Barwick

The Two Pence Servant

'Frank! Get me my pillow!' shouted Cleopatra.
'Yes, Miss,' Frank, one of her servants, said cautiously. This would go on for hours and hours. One day, when he was on his break, he got together the servant army and he came up with a cunning plan. 'Tomorrow, we will all go in there and get what we deserve!' exclaimed Frank. So they did.
After they told Cleopatra, she realised that it was really mean to only give them two pence every day and she should have been nicer. She gave them lots more money and wasn't as bossy.

Charley Hurst (9)
Barley Fields Primary School, Ingleby Barwick

Divorced, Beheaded, Died

Sentenced to her death on the 19th May 1536,
convicted of treason and adultery.

Anne Boleyn had caught the eye of Henry VIII. A
French, educated, beautiful daughter of a viscount,
Anne was unable to give Henry the son he desired.
So, within three years, he had lost interest in Anne,
having already allowed his eyes to look in the
direction of Jane Seymour.

Henry wanted Anne gone, so he plotted to have her
executed. Rumours of adultery and treason were
spread to make it easier to have her executed.
Divorced, beheaded, died...

Emily Atkinson (10)
Barley Fields Primary School, Ingleby Barwick

Anglo-Saxon Revenge

Guthrum stared at the cowering man crouched by the glowing embers of the fire. The peasant woman sobbed and beat the man with a gnarled stick. She shouted, 'You've burned our bread cakes. You're useless!'

That can't be King Alfred, thought Guthrum, dragging his huge, bloodied axe through the misty swamp. 'He's dead.' Guthrum smirked and turned back into the dark, reedy swamp, rejoining his army. Fireflies from the reeds settled on the cowering man's head and glowed like a crown. Two years later, a vanquished Guthrum knelt before a Saxon king. Looking up, he remembered with surprise, burned cakes!

Brooke Hills (8)
Barley Fields Primary School, Ingleby Barwick

Oh Boy!

It was a bright, sunny day when Jane Seymour and Henry were preparing for their baby in the castle. Jane was very worried about what Henry was going to do to her if she didn't have a boy.

Later that day, Henry was about to tell her what would happen but just then she froze. She was shaking. Then she gulped. He said, 'If you don't have a boy, you will see what will happen.'

Finally, she had a boy called Edward. Everyone celebrated but Jane collapsed. Everyone gasped in shock. They didn't know what happened to her.

Faith Baxendale (10)
Barley Fields Primary School, Ingleby Barwick

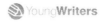

Victorians

A long time ago, there lived a queen named Queen Victoria. Queen Victoria had a very hard life because she had to make sure everything was going smoothly.

She was born on the 24th May 1819 in Kensington Palace, London. Queen Victoria became the queen on 20th June 1837 and died on 22nd January 1901.

Queen Victoria married a handsome and dashing man named Prince Albert. The castle was completely full, even though it was a big house. It was full because Queen Victoria gave birth to nine children, five girls and four sweet, kind boys.

Sumaya Hussain (9)
Barley Fields Primary School, Ingleby Barwick

The Mummies Are Coming

In the middle of the night, I woke up because of the splashing noise that I heard and my brother did too, as well as my parents. We all went out and went near the river. We saw somebody rowing on a boat. We didn't know who it was, but when the boat came nearer, we saw it was a mummy! The mummy got off the boat and said, 'Hello, I am here to take children away.'
We said, 'Well don't take us.'
But in the middle of the night when we were asleep, the mummy took us!

Jaehui Jang (7)
Barley Fields Primary School, Ingleby Barwick

Takkar And The Mysterious Hole

Every day when hunting with his tribe, young Takkar would pass a mysterious looking hole. The tribe master warned Takkar never to go near the hole as it possessed evil powers.

One day, when hunting, curiosity got the better of Takkar and he went near the hole. It swallowed him up and transported him to a strange world. There were children all wearing the same blue animal skins. They were running on the muga. Takkar didn't feel safe mixing with this new tribe so he chose to hide on the roof all day and caused mischief through the school at night.

Isabella Cooksey-Newlove (8)
Barley Fields Primary School, Ingleby Barwick

The Crown Of Cleopatra

Long ago in ancient Egypt, King Tutankhamun made an announcement to all Egyptians that he was going to give up his throne to his younger sister, Cleopatra. But he also said that once she was dead she'd be sent for mummification. She was terrified.

In the middle of the day, she fell into a hidden tomb under the palace. To get out she needed to find the pharaoh's crown for her crowning by crossing the trap of hieroglyphics about the mummy's death. Finally, she escaped in time for her coronation. At the end of the day she was crowned.

Maisie Smith (9)
Barley Fields Primary School, Ingleby Barwick

The Princess And The Rat

Once upon a time, there lived Princess Ella and she was 93. Imagine being 93 and a princess! How crazy! Ella had two great grandchildren, twins, a boy and a girl. The boy was called Ryan and the girl was called Lauren. It was summer so they went to their holiday home on the Isle of Wight, Osborne House.

One day, they were feeling cheeky and put a rat in their great grandmother's bed and ran down to Swiss Cottage. They were playing happily when they turned around to see their great grandmother glaring at them. They were in trouble!

Tara Jean Mogg (8)
Barley Fields Primary School, Ingleby Barwick

The Battlefield

The wind whistled deep down into the bottom of the endless dark trenches as Timothy Brown crawled out with a frown on his face. As he ran, he could almost feel the deep pain emanating from his fellow soldiers. The bullets flew past his head and ricocheted off the trench walls. Timothy realised they were losing the battle. Suddenly, he felt a sheer rush of pain flowing through his body and everything went dark.

When he eventually opened his eyes, he realised he was at home, tucked up in his comfy bed and it was all just a dream.

Charlie Watson (10)
Barley Fields Primary School, Ingleby Barwick

Ancient Egypt Adventures

Once, in ancient Egypt, there was an ancient guard called Bill. One day, Bill was checking the ancient tomb where the great Cleopatra was kept. Bill found out that a mummy was on the loose. He decided to have a meeting.

The next day, the Egyptians had a huge search and everyone in Egypt joined in to find the mummy. It took a long time. Eventually, after hours of running around, the Egyptians caught the mummy and put it back in its tomb. The king decided to have a party to celebrate catching the mummy. The people were happy.

Mia Atkinson (8)
Barley Fields Primary School, Ingleby Barwick

Diamond Dig

A family called the Uggs lived in a gloomy cave. Whilst out hunting, they found a volcano full of sparkling crystals. Daddy Ugg used a diamond pickaxe to gather the shimmering jewels.
'Dinosaur!' shouted Dad. A gigantic, fierce-looking beast ran towards them. 'Quick, run!' screamed Dad.
They ran through the deep, damp, dark forest until they approached a corner near to a cliff edge. Dad stopped. The dinosaur, however, continued and fell off the cliff into a deep blue river. He was never seen again.

Abigail Prudhoe (7)
Barley Fields Primary School, Ingleby Barwick

The Stone Age Saga

In 60,000BC, snow was falling from the sky and Pig and Stig were huddled together trying to keep warm. Stig had an excellent idea. He rubbed two sticks together and after a short while, a fire started. Stig said, 'I'm so hungry! Let's go eat!' Pig and Stig went searching for food with their flint spears they made earlier. Finally, they found food. Actually, it was a T-rex. Stig threw his spear into its heart and blood leaked out. The brave pig stabbed it with her spear to make sure it was dead.

Aaron Tuffnell (8)

Barley Fields Primary School, Ingleby Barwick

Mummified Dreams

Me and my dog, Tate, were walking along through the village when for the first time I noticed a strange looking tree. Built around it was a walled garden. Tate ran off towards it and I ran off after him. I gasped as what I found was a maze. I went this way and that way, peeping up were funny looking creatures. I followed a scent which could only be described as sweet-smelling chocolate. Suddenly, from out of nowhere, was a mummy...
Ding, ding! 'My alarm! Ah, it was all a dream!'

Daisy Stonehouse (9)
Barley Fields Primary School, Ingleby Barwick

Tommy's Horrible Disaster

One glorious day, Tommy set out to work at his new job in the deep, dark mine. Despite Tommy being only 14 years old, he still had to earn money for his poor family. When Tommy arrived at work, his manager addressed him in an impolite way. After that, Tommy put his helmet on and went down to the deep mine.

The next day, Tommy put his helmet on and went into the mine. He was chopping coal off when, suddenly, his axe slipped and cut off his finger. His mum came and rushed him to hospital...

Louie Stephenson (9)
Barley Fields Primary School, Ingleby Barwick

Titanic

Today is the best day ever because the new ship, the Titanic, is setting sail to New York. I am about to get on the ship, I am so excited. A staff member of the ship carries our bags for us and shows us our room. My mum is amazed by the room and my dad is starting to decorate the room already.
It has been two days on the Titanic and I am on the top deck. I see an iceberg coming towards us. I am quite scared in case we're hit. The iceberg is getting closer and closer...

Grace Neal (9)
Barley Fields Primary School, Ingleby Barwick

Mystery Man

When I was young, me and my best friend went to our town's dam. While we were there, an earthquake struck. My friend was in the middle of it. Ten years later, I was walking home when I saw a strange figure in black. For the next few weeks I saw him. I decided I needed to find out who he was. I followed him as far as he went but as I got to the river he was gone with no trace. I got home to find him in my front garden. Then he was gone. Then I saw him...

Harry Worton (9)
Barley Fields Primary School, Ingleby Barwick

England Are Undefeated

In 1939, Adolf Hitler and his German army decided to declare World War II and they invaded Poland. This war lasted for six years and ended in 1945. During this period, there were almost eleven million people killed, known as the Holocaust. England and France became allies and declared war on Germany. People became hungry as shops and supplies were targeted and rations started in the UK. Hitler then decided to invade Russia which was down as Operation Barbarossa. In 1942, Auschwitz and the mass killing of Jewish people started. In 1945, Hitler committed suicide and Germany surrendered to England.

Max Platts (7)
Barley Fields Primary School, Ingleby Barwick

War At The Village

Exhausted and breathless, I sprinted as fast as my arrows whilst the silhouette pounded after me. The cottages were burnt to a crisp and the matted grass was ashen. Just then, I stumbled over a dead body. Unable to pause and acknowledge this wounded shell, I staggered to my feet. For the briefest moment the atmosphere grew mysteriously quiet. Suddenly, I heard a peculiar sound coming from the nearby bushes; whispered words I couldn't understand. My entire body froze whilst one eye dared to glimpse out of its corner. The whispers stopped dead. The leaves shuddered. There it was...

Emma Pickup (9)
Barley Fields Primary School, Ingleby Barwick

Mummy's Meeting

In 1485, the Tudors were living in a castle with disgusting walls and spiderwebs all over the floor. An unexpected mummy approached. The Tudors' hearts were pounding with fear and they froze in shock. Within a second, the mummy noticed the castle starting to crumble in the distance. Behind him stood a Tudor skeleton with bloodied bones and a scary skull. The skeleton lived in a haunted house and you could see the bloody footprints leading from the archway. Furthermore, the skeleton had seen the mummy and was wondering if they could meet. A few minutes later, they met and...

Lucy Fletcher (10)
Barley Fields Primary School, Ingleby Barwick

The Mythical Olympics

In the year 776BC, the leaders of ancient Greece decided to hold the first Olympic games, inviting all of the mythical creatures. The games were held at Sarpedon with the first event being the Minotaur versus Medusa at snakes and ladders. At the Olympics, the Minotaur went first and rolled three sixes in a row. Everyone celebrated whilst Medusa sneaked one of her snakes under the Minotaur's counter, moving him back to the start. The referee said, 'You're disqualified.' Medusa became angry. She turned him and all of the other creatures to stone. Guess who won?

Louis Latcham (9)
Barley Fields Primary School, Ingleby Barwick

Fright At The Museum!

Here I am on my first trip to the National History Museum. Room one, Ancient Egypt. I'm staring at a mummy. It is staring back at me. Did it just move? I don't like this, time to leave. I head off to a new room: Ancient Greece. Another mummy! This can't be. I'm out of here! Quickly, I run down the corridor. Where can I go? There! Into the safety of Ancient Rome. Surely no mummies here. But what's this? I can't believe it. This can't be happening, impossible. Another mummy! But wait, not another mummy... *it's the same mummy!*

Ruby Grace Simpson (10)
Barley Fields Primary School, Ingleby Barwick

Wingless Wonders

Seats of Wembley Stadium filled with 46,924 nervous fans on July 30th 1966, a historical day that England will never forget. England took on their rivals, Germany, for the World Cup finals. It was thrilling throughout with both teams thirsty for glory. Germany scored first, only 12 minutes in and England knew they had an almighty battle to fight. But we had a secret weapon! Geoff Hurst and Martin Peters scored an amazing four goals. The final goal, sent like a rocket, hit the back of the net like a cannonball. The crowd went wild. England 4, Germany 2!

Joseph Barron (8)
Barley Fields Primary School, Ingleby Barwick

Attire In One's Eyes

Colours obstructing my vision. Habiliment hung in order across the vague walls that confine one's mind into thinking it desires the one object that will make no blessedness to their future at all. What am I doing in this place? After all, my language that was once slang is now spoken of in English and history. But I'm another forgotten soul. The attire chosen by these people is not for my pleasure but I feast my eyes upon the children that beg for one's outfit so they can follow the crowd. I, Shakespeare, am not one for this absurd environment.

Jessica Thompson (10)
Barley Fields Primary School, Ingleby Barwick

The Monster Beside Us

I woke with a strange feeling in my tummy. Suddenly, the ground beneath my feet began to shake and the sound of tiles smashing rang in my ears. Carefully, I stumbled to the window, looking into the distance. I could see clouds of ash billowing out of Mount Vesuvius. I'd seen this many times before but the feeling that something was wrong wouldn't leave me. *Crash!* The sound startled me and my room lit up with a blinding flash. Fire surrounded me, hot lava rocks lit up the sky like fireworks. Vesuvius was becoming a monster greedy for blood!

Aiden Colmer (8)

Barley Fields Primary School, Ingleby Barwick

The Guarded Assassin

A Roman guard is diligently stood by his post, carrying out his duty. He has been instructed by the emperor to watch out for an assassin who is rumoured to be in the city. It is exhausting work and the guard struggles to stay awake. Suddenly, he is startled by a rustle in the nearby bush. A dark, shadowy figure lurks in the moonlight, but in an instant it vanishes. *Did I really see that?* thought the guard, puzzled. The night passes without incident, or so the guard thinks. In daylight the emperor appears, dagger in hand. What's happened?

Jack Macdonald (8)
Barley Fields Primary School, Ingleby Barwick

The Kidnapped Son Of King Arthur

Kidnapped! The son of King Arthur had been kidnapped. The country was devastated. Arthur ordered his finest men to help him find his son. They put on their finest armour and gathered their strongest horses. They searched the kingdom far and wide. After days of searching, they came across the dragon of Mount Black's cave. At last they had found Arthur's son. He was weak but still alive. In the blackness of the cave were big, red flaming eyes, bloodied teeth and razor-sharp claws! It was the dragon! Would they survive or would it be a sticky ending?

Matthew Thompson (9)
Barley Fields Primary School, Ingleby Barwick

Blazing City

Suddenly, I was awoken by loud crashing, shouting and screams of terror. Father ran into my room just as I noticed the roof beam had fallen and the house was ablaze. Mother, Father, my brother Seth and I held onto each other as we hurried out of the flaming, ash-covered door. The smoke pierced our eyes and seemed to burn our noses and throats. Outside, the streets were chaotic with frightened, confused, injured people. The night sky shone above us like a million rubies. The smoke and heat were overpowering. London Bridge was devoured by the River Thames.

Oliver McMahon (9)
Barley Fields Primary School, Ingleby Barwick

The Great Fire

The famous Samuel Pepys was in his house in London. Suddenly, he saw a fire coming down the street and he got really, really scared. He couldn't breathe. His heart raced as he ran around in circles panicking. 'What can I do?' The fire was getting closer at an uncontrollable speed. 'I don't know how to save myself!' The air was misty with heat and smoke. The fire was getting bigger and the flames were getting stronger. He ran in panic to his back garden. Finally, he realised what he had to do; he buried his wine and cheese. Relief!

Samuel Law (8)
Barley Fields Primary School, Ingleby Barwick

The Curse Of The Mummy!

As the school bus approached ancient Egypt, the sunrise beamed over the pyramids. Gazing nervously out of the window, Poppy laughed at her friend's joke about the curse of the mummy. The bus screeched to a halt and the children ran excitedly into the room. But not Poppy... she saw a small, golden pyramid and felt compelled to go in. As she put her hand on the hieroglyphics, the door opened with a bang. Poppy went inside. There were lots of people and a large sarcophagus. Everyone ignored her. The lid flew open and a dirty mummy began to climb out...

Erin Barnfather (8)
Barley Fields Primary School, Ingleby Barwick

Romans Attack Labyrinth

I was peacefully walking around the labyrinth for the second time. I softly walked back through the entrance. From both sides I could see the Romans charging straight at me, holding shields and battleaxes. I was terrified and started running swiftly around the labyrinth with only my bare fists to fight them off. I was terrified so I kept on running. One quarter of the Romans followed me, dashing around the labyrinth. As the Romans came to a halt, they started marching back towards their heavily guarded village. How did the labyrinth hold up? Was it OK?

Owen Snell (9)

Barley Fields Primary School, Ingleby Barwick

A Day At A Victorian School

It was a bright, sunny Friday morning. Francesca and Daisy were happily skipping to school. They started to write on their slates, then the teacher said, 'Tidy up.' There was a knock on the door. It was Queen Victoria. The queen looked very carefully at Francesca and Daisy. Daisy won an award from the queen because she did a good job at cleaning the slates. It was a trophy! The children sat at their desks and asked the queen, 'What's it like to be a queen?' It was home time and Daisy and Francesca were laughing as they went home.

Holly Salt (7)
Barley Fields Primary School, Ingleby Barwick

Beasts Are Destroying

A long time ago, a bear howled and growled and eventually escaped from a pyramid. Sand flew along. I looked closely and it was a huge bear. I warned the village. Screaming people, yelling crowds, but in the distance came a fierce howl. All was not lost for this man called Jimmy wasn't scared at all. Thunder hit, lightning crashed. *Roar! Roar!* It was like a nightmare. Jimmy went to the beast and hit him with his sword. Now the beast was howling with pain. Then the beast ran away. Now the village lived happily ever after. Bye-bye, beast!

Louis Wilkinson (8)
Barley Fields Primary School, Ingleby Barwick

The Creeps

In a mysterious forest where nobody had explored, there lived a witch and a kid who hated each other. One sunny, scorching morning, the kid found a mouldy pond. As quick as a flash, Jack the kid found out it was the witch's new home. The witch saw Jack and cackled wickedly. Jack dived in the pond and stole a poster from the witch. After that, the witch bolted out of the pond and darted for Jack. She wailed, 'I will give you money.' Shortly after, they suddenly strangely became friends and they visited each other every day and night.

Jody Noble (8)
Barley Fields Primary School, Ingleby Barwick

Erik The Red - The Discovery Of Greenland

Erik and his wife boarded their Viking vessel to leave their home in search of new lands. A few weeks into that journey, they noticed black clouds rolling in. They battened down the hatches. Suddenly, it got very dark. They looked up and saw the biggest wave they had ever seen heading straight for them. They went below deck and braced themselves. The wave hit and rocked the ship all over. They began taking on water. They were all scared. They made it to morning. At first light they spotted land. They named it Greenland and made it their home.

Jack Howen (8)
Barley Fields Primary School, Ingleby Barwick

The Cabin Boy's Discovery

It was a dark, stormy night aboard the Blue Diamond. Jack knew this was his chance to steal some bread. As he crept along the ship's deck, the wooden planks creaked with every step Jack took. He reached the galley and headed straight towards the bread but, suddenly, heard the cook waking up. At that moment, he was engulfed with fear. Trembling, he opened the cupboard but, to his surprise, it didn't contain any bread. However, he found a rolled-up piece of paper. Slowly opening it, he realised it was a map... a treasure map!

Joseph McCulloch (9)
Barley Fields Primary School, Ingleby Barwick

Modern Warfare

The English army go on a mission to the pyramids of Giza and uncover the secret of the undead army and their leader is the famous pharaoh king, Tutankhamun. The English leader, Captain Blunder Bus, and his modern day army fight the ancient mummified warriors and clash together and form a colossal battle between alive and dead. The battle lasts a whole month and many, many lives are lost. The army bring Chinooks, Lancaster bombers and Apaches and tanks but mummies just keep flooding out! But.. twelve men come with a huge nuclear bomb...

James Roebuck (8)
Barley Fields Primary School, Ingleby Barwick

England Vs Germany

I was really excited for England versus Germany. I was really hoping England would score a goal. The players were ready to go on the pitch. Suddenly, I heard this massive bang. Every single person there was absolutely stunned and shocked. There was a moment of silence and the next thing anyone knew, gladiators and slaves were running on the pitch. Everyone tried to get out but too many people couldn't because Wembley Stadium was jammed. The gladiators started to fight all the slaves and the battle was on. To be honest, it was very good.

William Braithwaite (9)
Barley Fields Primary School, Ingleby Barwick

Princess Matilda

When Matilda was plotting her plans to kill her enemy, she grabbed her weapon, extra sharp, extra big. She decided to plan her disguise to kill. People were looking at her strangely whilst running away but she looked back at them creepily. Finally, her enemy, Lily, came round the block and *stab!* While Lily was on the floor people were screaming while Matilda was laughing. After a while, Matilda wanted to kill Queen Victoria, so she stole the crown and was queen. Five years later, Matilda was killed by the British guards of London.

Annabelle Shipton (8)
Barley Fields Primary School, Ingleby Barwick

Sweet Revolution

As I walked down the bloody path, I witnessed riots. Out of the mist I saw the biggest castle, possibly ever. It was my last hope of survival. Desperately, I ran to it. There was no answer. It was unlocked. I went in to find a kitchen full of cake. I was famished. I needed something to eat. Slowly, I walked towards a stunning cake. Without thinking, I devoured every crumb. At that moment, a towering shadow cast over me. It was Marie Antoinette! As she was about to speak, countless silhouettes moved towards us. A new revolution was born...

Zahraa Adam (10)
Barley Fields Primary School, Ingleby Barwick

The Waiting Game

I sat nervously on the dusty floor. I was trembling with fear and my heart was pumping faster and faster as each minute passed. I had trained for this nearly all of my life. Was I ready to fight as the first woman gladiator? Suddenly, a strange figure appeared and walked towards me. He viciously thrust a sword and shield into my hands. They were wet and damp and made my fingers tingle. I clutched them tightly. Time was running out! Slowly, the heavy metal gate rose. I took a deep breath and stepped into the light. The crowd went wild...

Elizabeth Carr (9)
Barley Fields Primary School, Ingleby Barwick

Forbidden Fruit

Skipping through the busy village market, the sun blazed down on Mary. The smell of food made her tummy rumble really loud. In the corner of her eye she spotted a very red, juicy apple. Mary couldn't resist. She wanted the fruit. She convinced herself to steal it from the old man's stall. Grabbing the apple, she bolted through the street until she could no longer run. So she picked some berries to eat whilst getting her breath back. Crouching behind a barrel, she looked up and saw two piercing eyes glaring down. Who was it?

Izzie McCue (8)
Barley Fields Primary School, Ingleby Barwick

The Fight Of Doom!

The sky was as dark as black paint and the family lit their lanterns, ready for battle. Their emerald-green treasure was safely buried from the fierce Viking. The Viking was prepared with his axe and he was angry for battle. He had a pale face, scratches, cuts and was covered in blood. The Viking was going to steal the family's treasure because he wanted to rule the kingdom and be rich. He searched the village for the house that was ready to fight. The Viking thought he would win but the strong family had never lost a fight...

Erin Gauchi (7)
Barley Fields Primary School, Ingleby Barwick

The Greek Times

Once upon a time, a boy was walking, he then fell through a mysterious sink hole. After he fell through, he woke up in a strange place that resembled ancient Greece. When he looked around it was very loud and bustling with people dressed in ancient attire. The local people also thought he was strange-looking as he was dressed in a T-shirt and jeans. As he walked around, people were staring at him. He was interested in the Colosseum. He saw a gladiator battle. As the audience ducked, a shield hit him in the head. He was out cold...

Kelvin Ho (9)
Barley Fields Primary School, Ingleby Barwick

Oliver's Day Out

My name is Oliver Borrow and I'm a World War II pilot. My Spitfire aeroplane is called Plotto. One summer day, I was flying my plane when my engine suddenly stopped. Plotto began to spiral out of control towards the ground. I jumped out and pulled my parachute cord but it didn't open properly. I continued to fall. That's when I spotted the roof of a large building. I closed my eyes and braced myself ready to crash through the roof. A few seconds later, there was a loud crash! I woke up and I was in a mattress factory.

Daisy Pryde (9)
Barley Fields Primary School, Ingleby Barwick

Viking Invasion

The sun rose, the brightness startled me and woke me from my daze. My arms felt heavy and sweat ran down my forehead under my helmet. On the horizon was a beautiful monastery, lit up by the sun. We were nearly there! The land in front of me was a mystery. I was scared, nervous and excited at the same time. I looked around at my fellow rowing mates who were sweating too from rowing for days on end. The boat which I had called home, silently approached the island. I waited nervously and then I heard the command... 'Charge!'

Charlotte Glaister (9)
Barley Fields Primary School, Ingleby Barwick

The Vikings Have Landed

I have just witnessed a scene that no human should have to endure. Fearing for my life, I run like the speed of lightning to hide. My heart is pumping so rapidly, I feel my chest will explode. Sweat is oozing from my pores. I am in the most appalling danger! I make it to a room where I hide, unseen under straw. As the window has no glass, from outside I hear the screams of monks as they are horrifically and brutally murdered. It is the 8th June 793AD. I'm in Lindisfarne monastery. *The Vikings have landed!* Help me!

Jack Mallett (8)
Barley Fields Primary School, Ingleby Barwick

The Curse Of Tutankhamun

Me and my brother were walking along in the hot sun, in the Valley of the Kings. Suddenly, I heard a crumbling noise, which started to get louder and louder. My heart was pounding. 'Aaahhh!' I had fallen into a hole. It was not just any ordinary hole, it was the tomb of Tutankhamun. Just then, the wind started to howl my name! I knew something must have been wrong. Then, sand started filling the hole until I was about to disappear under it. My brother tried to help me. It must have been the curse of Tutankhamun...

Annabelle Ryan (8)
Barley Fields Primary School, Ingleby Barwick

Christopher Columbus And The Wicked Pirates

Christopher Columbus was on a new adventure when suddenly he came across an island. It was beautiful, like nothing he had ever seen before. He thought to himself, *what could I call this land?* All of a sudden pirates jumped out of their boats and attacked Christopher Columbus and his crew. The pirates weren't interested in the land, just their money and shiny gold. It took everything Columbus' crew had to fight off the pirates but they claimed the victory and went on to live on the land and call it their home.

Milly Johnston-Wild (8)
Barley Fields Primary School, Ingleby Barwick

Egyptian Wonderland

One day, a girl named Jazzy set off in an aeroplane to Egypt. She fell asleep on the way and had an extraordinary dream. In the dream she was in Egypt. Jazzy met a pharaoh named Malorn who told her the way to his castle. On the way she saw a sign that said: 'Egyptian Wonderland'. Jazzy went inside and there were a lot of food stalls and entertainment stalls. When she left she saw King Malorn outside the 'Egyptian Wonderland'. She finally went to the exit of Egypt. Jazzy woke up and found out she was in Egypt.

Lily Beck (9)
Barley Fields Primary School, Ingleby Barwick

Queen In Black

After many years of happy marriage and nine children, her most beloved husband sadly died. Prince Albert had been her constant companion and she was devastated by his death. After that she wore black clothes for the rest of her long, lonely life as a sign of mourning. Her least unhappy part of her life, after Albert had sadly died was when she spent time in Scotland with a gentleman named John Brown. They used to go out on horseback together. When Queen Victoria died, she asked for colourful flowers but not too much black.

Jemma Rigby (8)
Barley Fields Primary School, Ingleby Barwick

Cleopatra's Bad Day!

One cold morning as the sun was rising, a very loud scream came from the temple. Cleopatra had nits! She sprang out of bed to get into her milk bath. She jumped in with a splash! The milk had turned sour! Her servants were always there to help her but today they were all sick! She tried lighting a fire to make charcoal for her eye make-up. She failed, never having done it before. She tried getting dressed. Again, it was too confusing for her! Cleopatra went back to bed thinking this was the best day ever... not! Goodnight!

Lucia Raine (9)
Barley Fields Primary School, Ingleby Barwick

Who Did It?

It was two o'clock in the morning when Henry awoke. Just then he heard a sound. The sound came from downstairs. Henry put on his clothes and ran downstairs. He walked into the living room to find his wife dead. When he looked beside him, he found that the window had been smashed. Next to her was a knife. When he looked at her, he found that her chest was bleeding. He gave another glance at the knife. He wondered what had happened. Henry looked out of the window. Just then, a man in black walked into the living room...

Alana McGee (10)
Barley Fields Primary School, Ingleby Barwick

Ancient Greeks' Mycenaean Civilization

A long time ago, in a textile industry, there was a builder named Ken Stephenson. He was building a Mycenaean archaeological site in Greece when Glen Vanzeller came along (Ken's friend). He was an engineer. Then the builder had a really good idea that he would take his friend Glen to help him build a Greek temple. He had loads of building materials but he still didn't know what he would build it out of or how to sculpture it. But then, in the middle of building it, he ran out of materials he needed to build with.

Imogen Smith (10)
Barley Fields Primary School, Ingleby Barwick

Erik's Voyage

The freezing water of the sea splashed over my rough feet. The man sat behind was sick on me. Our boat was rocking from side to side. My arms felt dead as they had been rowing for many days. I daren't look up, I felt queasy. A storm fired up behind us. 'Where are we?' I cried. The storm controlled us and our boat. Where was it taking us? Suddenly, as if by magic, Mother Nature heard our cries and the sea calmed down. The mist cleared. I saw a woman staring at us in shock. 'The Vikings!' she screamed.

Lauren Gill (10)
Barley Fields Primary School, Ingleby Barwick

The Gladiator's Surprise

Once, there was a very fierce Roman gladiator. He was the fiercest of all the gladiators and everyone was very afraid of him except for his little girl. One day, they went to a very big market and everyone seemed very scared of him. He couldn't understand why as it was his day off from scaring people. His little girl kept saying to him that he was a ghost, but he didn't believe her. A few minutes later, he looked in the mirror and he only saw his galea hovering in the air! He couldn't believe his own eyes!

Ava Barber (8)
Barley Fields Primary School, Ingleby Barwick

The Pharaoh And The Tomb!

One day there was a pharaoh called Rameses and he was a greedy person. He decided to walk outside and suddenly saw a secret tomb. He went inside and saw some hidden treasure such as gold. He wanted to keep it all for himself, so he tried to carry as much as he could. Out of nowhere a mummy appeared and got angry at the pharaoh for stealing the treasure. Then it started to chase him all around. Since that day, he was never seen again so his brother became the new pharaoh. This shows that greediness leads to problems.

Zahra Mobin (8)
Barley Fields Primary School, Ingleby Barwick

The Mischievous Time Machine

Once, there was a girl called Grace. She lived in the Victorian period and she was an inventor. On a chilling winter night, Queen Victoria came and asked the inventor to make her a time machine. The inventor made the time machine but made it wrong. People from the village heard about the time machine and asked her to make them one. When the Queen went in it, she chose the Stone Age but there was a terrible mistake. It exploded! Nobody knows what happened to her, but ten years later, she still hasn't been found.

Grace Wanless (9)
Barley Fields Primary School, Ingleby Barwick

The Unusual Desert

One cold winter's day, in a deserted desert there was a person, standing, not moving at all. Twelve hours later, the unusual figure started walking towards a well that had suddenly appeared in the distance. The person was amazed to find a coin in their pocket. So he or she threw it into the well. In a flash, a full moon appeared in the sky and lots of mummies came out of nowhere. Then they all started to walk towards the person and... *boom!* All had disappeared except for the person whose name was...

Lola Painter (9)
Barley Fields Primary School, Ingleby Barwick

The Smallest Room

It was dark. My parents said it would soon be over as I tried to make myself comfortable in the cramped space. My eyes felt heavy as I drifted off to sleep but jumped as the sound of deafening bangs and loud rumblings exploded outside the door. My mother squeezed me tight as the smell of smoke grew stronger. The sound of bells got louder as a dim light appeared through the door. We left the safety of the cupboard under the stairs to find our house was destroyed. We were alive at least and the air raid was over.

Emily Clapton (10)
Barley Fields Primary School, Ingleby Barwick

The Mischievous Mummy

Once upon a time, there lived a young boy called George. He lived in London. George flew from London to Egypt. When he got there, he found a pyramid so he went in. Happily, he skipped inside and guess what was there? A coffin! As silly as a cheeky monkey, he opened it and there was a... mummy! Only one of his ribbons was falling. Therefore he pulled and the mummy quickly vanished! He came out of the really big pyramid and couldn't stop thinking about it. This was a memory that would never ever be forgotten.

Sadie Savage
Barley Fields Primary School, Ingleby Barwick

Archaeologist Discovers About Ancient Egypt

Evan Taylor was an American archaeologist from New York. He was asked to go to Egypt to study ancient Egyptian life. He slept in a tent beneath the pyramids before exploring the mummy's tomb. In the morning, a T-rex chased him into the pyramid, but he managed to fight it off with a spear. Exploring deeper, he found the mummy's treasure but it was very heavy so he tied it to the T-rex and pulled it out of the tomb. He returned to America a rich hero with an unusual pet called Rex with a large appetite.

Alex Buckingham (7)
Barley Fields Primary School, Ingleby Barwick

A Creepy Adventure

A young boy was always interested in the pyramids near the market and today his plan was to look inside. He saw a doorway and went inside the mysterious pyramid. The creaky door shut behind him to make it really dark and he felt scared. He tried to open the door again but it was jammed. He walked further into the pitch-black pyramid and could feel the air getting colder and colder. Suddenly, he saw a dim light at the end of the corridor. He walked into the room and came face-to-face with a terrifying mummy!

Alfie Baker (8)
Barley Fields Primary School, Ingleby Barwick

The Ancient Tomb

In ancient Egypt, in an ancient pyramid, there was a dusty, ancient tomb guarded by a mummy and a pharaoh. At night the tumbleweeds were tumbling everywhere, pebbles went everywhere, cacti started growing and water started to fade away. Inside the temple was a treasure hunter who found the dusty tomb and he got the treasure, but when he got the treasure, the leader of the pharaohs came! Then he had to get out, but how? Then he had a plan, he had a pickaxe so he could mine out! He escaped with the treasure.

Rehan Ashraf (8)
Barley Fields Primary School, Ingleby Barwick

Deadly Mummy

A long time ago in the nineteenth century, there lived a deadly mummy and a young girl named Bloom. In an old castle the mummy lurked. Bloom was on a day trip in the old castle. All of a sudden, the lights went out. From nowhere, the mummy appeared. Bloom had to react fast. She found a key to the mummy's chamber. She opened the door and pushed the deadly mummy in. She locked the door behind the mummy and then escaped from the castle. Bloom posted the key through the letterbox and left, never to return.

Tanwyn Smith (8)
Barley Fields Primary School, Ingleby Barwick

The Battle

My heart was pounding. Could we really win this battle? The odds were stacked against us. If we won, fame and glory would be ours but if we lost, it would cost us our lives. I couldn't believe this was actually happening. My armour suddenly felt so heavy and I was breathing so quickly, I thought I was going to faint. However, there was no time to change my mind. I could already sense our opponent was here. I gathered up my courage, held my sword aloft and charged to my destiny. I never felt more alive!

Nathan Easby (9)
Barley Fields Primary School, Ingleby Barwick

Henry VIII

Five hundred years ago, in the Tudor times, King Henry VIII ruled the country. At that time, because he had the best of food and expensive French wine, he put on a large amount of weight. The only thing Henry could fit into was his nightshirt because none of his clothes would fit him. When he went out on his duties in the village, the people would stare and call him names about the way he looked and what he was wearing. Due to all this negativity, he became less visible among his friends until his death.

Poppy Ashley (10)
Barley Fields Primary School, Ingleby Barwick

Blood, Sweat And Tears

Sweat and blood dripped down my face. I didn't know it was mine. I was tired and numb. It had been a long and hard battle between two groups of great Viking warriors. I looked out across a field of motionless bodies. Some were once my friends, others were foes. Amongst the silence I could hear a groan. As I struggled to walk towards the noise, mud squelched under my feet. As I got closer, I realised I was not the only survivor. As I got closer, I noticed it was my best friend, Wilfred, who was there.

Dominic Hopton (8)
Barley Fields Primary School, Ingleby Barwick

The Gold That Belonged To The Sphinx

The night was dark as I stared above, but what I could see was the sphinx. I bravely entered as traps were hidden in there, until one shot an arrow. *Bam!* It hit a wall right near me! *That was close!* I thought. Suddenly, I could see water was guiding me somewhere. I wondered where. Surely this was bad. There it was, gleaming in the light of the trapped area, a chunk of gold! I was rich! I took one piece, but lava arose. I put it back but it didn't stop so I ran and managed to escape.

Elliott Wright (9)

Barley Fields Primary School, Ingleby Barwick

Anina's Story

It was quiet, but only for a moment. Suddenly, the sirens rang and me and my family ran for cover. We sat in the shelter for hours and hours and all we heard was the sound of booming bombs which were surrounding us. Usually I would get scared, but it has become a normal thing to me. Sometimes it happens at night. In the dark we usually go to the shelter. My parents have ration books. We get food every week. We get rations of butter, eggs, meat, sugar, jam and bread. My house and shelter were blown up...

Amelia Coates (9)
Barley Fields Primary School, Ingleby Barwick

The Mummy Strikes

Running as fast as her legs could carry her, she ran rapidly. Desperately, she tried to escape from the menacing mummy. Would she escape the evil monster behind her? All she could do now was hide. But where? Fortunately, she knew a place that no one else knew... the chambers. Creeping down the deadly chambers, she silently walked through the alleyways like a mouse. The charging mummy looked like the most vicious thing you have ever seen in your life. It grabbed her hand as tight as possible and then...

Evie Thompson (7)
Barley Fields Primary School, Ingleby Barwick

Iron Horse

It was a bright, sunny September day with a clear blue sky. I walked slowly and nervously towards the wooden cart with wheels made of iron. In front of me was a big, black iron machine that had massive wheels sat on a track. People were calling it an iron horse. Suddenly, a big, black cloud came out of the high chimney on the front of the black machine. Suddenly, it moved and everyone cheered loudly. Clanging, banging and in a cloud of smoke, we were off! Off on the first ever train going to Stockton.

Ava McCulloch (8)
Barley Fields Primary School, Ingleby Barwick

The English Jewel Hunter And The Creature

Forty centuries ago, there lived a man called Frank who decided to go to Egypt as a he was a jewel hunter. He started to travel on a big ship. The ship was going ten miles an hour. He needed to get there faster, so Frank found a speedboat and went twenty miles an hour. It took twelve hours to get to Egypt. When he arrived, he found tons of jewels. Suddenly, two red eyes appeared, then two claws. The creature was a mummy. It chased and chased him but he met a man who helped him get home safely.

Elleanor Waddington (8)

Barley Fields Primary School, Ingleby Barwick

A Walk In The Canyon

One thunderous afternoon, I was on a day trip to the Grand Canyon. I walked and walked. The scenery was spectacular. I heard a ferocious hiss from behind me. Suddenly, a ginormous T-rex jumped out of a bush next to me. I screamed as loud as I could for help but no one could hear. I ran for my life. Before long, I was right on the edge when the T-rex bared his razor-sharp teeth. I backed up. I was petrified! What could I do? There was another lightning strike. I saw its spiky claws. Was it the end?

Charlie Lythgoe (9)
Barley Fields Primary School, Ingleby Barwick

The Walking Dead

The sun shone on the dry, dusty sand which was being blown onto my eyes by the strong wind. I decided to enter a cave. It was pure darkness and I could barely see in front of me. As I got further in the cave, I could see a coffin covered in cobwebs and spiders. Feeling petrified, I walked up to it with caution. Bravely, I opened the lid. I put my hand in the coffin and touched a cold, rough material. Feeling frightened, I started to run, not realising I was being chased. *It was a mummy!*

Ben Mills (8)
Barley Fields Primary School, Ingleby Barwick

The Germans Are Coming

The rain was pouring but the Germans kept coming. I squeezed the trigger hard on my gun, but I missed. He was still coming. I squeezed again... nothing. The gun was empty! I was helpless. I lay back frozen in fear, hoping he would pass and think I was dead. But he didn't. He came into my bunker and searched us all, probably looking for guns or bombs. Out of nowhere, one of my colleagues came up behind the German and shot him in the back of the head. He fell to the floor in a pool of blood.

Lily Allcock (10)
Barley Fields Primary School, Ingleby Barwick

Mia And The Mummy

Riding home through the desert after a long day working at the market, something spooked my camel, throwing me off and landing me in a heap on hot sand. As I got up, I noticed a figure through the sandstorm. I could not believe my eyes. Frozen to the spot, the figure started to come closer. Petrified, I crept back, reaching for my camel. Suddenly, the figure approached me and I was face-to-face with a mummy. Sensing I was in danger, I jumped on my camel and rode as fast as I could to safety.

Isabelle McQuade (9)
Barley Fields Primary School, Ingleby Barwick

The Mummy Is Here!

I was on holiday in Egypt and me and my friend, Katie, were in the pyramid looking at all of the treasure. But as soon as night came, we were locked in. We were so scared. As we shivered, there was a creak and a door opened. A mummy came out! It grabbed me. It had dark, red eyes. I tried to wriggle out but it was so strong. We finally got out and silently crept away, holding each other firmly. The mummy was looking everywhere. We tiptoed to the other side and then the mummy ran towards us...

Emily Dixon (9)
Barley Fields Primary School, Ingleby Barwick

London's Burning

Once, there was a baker in the large city of London where he lived with his wife in a small shop on Pudding Lane. One day, the baker and his wife decided to make an extra loaf of bread, so the baker made the dough and placed it in the oven. Then, suddenly, huge spikes of flame burst out! He tried to put the fire out but it was no use, it kept spreading and spreading. The firemen caught a glimpse of the city and rushed right over. The husband and wife couldn't believe what had happened.

Emily Davidson (9)
Barley Fields Primary School, Ingleby Barwick

Tom The Champion

Finally, Tom's moment came. The referee blew his whistle for a penalty in the last five seconds. Tommy went and picked up the football. He had never been so scared, but Tommy could hear the thousands of dinosaur fans going silent. After he put the ball on the spot, Tom looked up to see Sharkan, the greatest pterodactyl goalkeeper ever. The referee blew his whistle. He took two steps back and he ran up to the ball and booted it... *Roar!* went the crowd. Tommy was the champion!

Benjamin Farrow (8)
Barley Fields Primary School, Ingleby Barwick

The Mystery Of Tutankhamun

Tutankhamun was walking around the pyramids when he saw a pyramid with a jewel on the tomb. He went inside. It was boring but then he saw some drawings saying: 'RIP Tutankhamun!' As soon as he saw them, he got scared and ran for his life. The door of the tomb closed and then everything went silent and black. He found some wood, so he made a fire. Then he felt something rather odd and screamed in shock because he was holding a mummy's hand. He raced out of the tomb and fell...

Max Edwards (9)
Barley Fields Primary School, Ingleby Barwick

The Tomb

In a dark and dimly lit tomb, the slaves set about their work of mummification, starting with the internal organs. Blood, brains and guts were everywhere! The slaves became hot and tired. They decided that they would have a sleep after they had finished the bandages. Only one slave was half awake as the rest slept. He was just about to close his eyes when, suddenly, the mummy stood up and walked towards the slave. At that moment, all the candles flickered, then went out. Was he dreaming?

Sam Patton (9)
Barley Fields Primary School, Ingleby Barwick

The Mummy Invasion!

The wind growled, the sand flew into my eyes as the mythical creature chased me. In the faraway distance, I could see a big wall blocking my way. When I reached the wall I stopped and stared. When the creature came really close, I ran for my life back the other way. When I got far away, it noticed me... It ran super fast to get me so I kept running. When the creature caught me up, it went in front of me to stop me and I saw it had bandages on it everywhere. Then I realised... mummy!

Emma Nary (8)
Barley Fields Primary School, Ingleby Barwick

The Treasure Hunter And The Hidden Mummy!

A long time ago, in a faraway country called Egypt, there lived a very adventurous treasure hunter. One day, the hunter found a pyramid. He looked around and saw a door, so he went in, without an inkling of fear. He wandered about inside the huge pyramid and found an old, dusty coffin. The hunter opened the coffin lid. Then, out came an alive mummy! Suddenly, the pyramid began to collapse and the hunter was stuck. Beside him, he found a rock. With the rock he got out. Finally, free!

Lily Webster (8)
Barley Fields Primary School, Ingleby Barwick

The Stone Age With Ugg

I was playing football with my friends. The ball went into the bushes, so I went to retrieve it. A voice called to me. I looked and saw a caveman staring at me. His name was Ugg. He offered me his hand and within a flash, I was sat in his cave with his family, who were hungry. Ugg gave me a weapon and went hunting for dinosaur meat. We crept up on this big dinosaur and I threw my spear towards it. It missed. The dinosaur roared and charged towards us with its large teeth snapping...

Harry Robson (9)
Barley Fields Primary School, Ingleby Barwick

Captain Cook's Cat

It was the middle of the night and I crept past all 100 sailors on the docks at Plymouth harbour. I reached out and jumped on the huge ship. I ran down to the hull of the ship and curled next to something warm and fell asleep. The next thing I knew I woke to a huge commotion, ran up to the deck and saw people fighting with swords. I was scared. One of the men said, 'Stop!' They were practising in case of a pirate attack. The captain told me I could stay on as his pet.

Ryan Mills (8)
Barley Fields Primary School, Ingleby Barwick

The Ancient Woman

A very long time ago Victoria, a pagan girl, decided to go to Stonehenge for a walk. She found a cave and walked further in than she had before. It got darker and darker until she couldn't see a thing. Suddenly, she fell into a hole. She was crying her eyes out. Then she saw a light shining into her eyes and looked up. There was a rope hanging down the tunnel. She grabbed it and pulled herself out. It was the longest day of the year. She told her family of her adventures.

Bonnie Bennett (8)

Barley Fields Primary School, Ingleby Barwick

The Egyptian T-Rex

James and his family were on holiday in Egypt, visiting the pyramids. As James headed towards the biggest pyramid, a door suddenly opened on the side of it. James walked nervously inside and there was a coffin shaped like a dinosaur. Suddenly, out jumped a huge T-rex with massive teeth. James ran for his life out the door as fast as he could. The door slammed shut behind him and hit the T-rex in the face and he fell back into the coffin. The lid banged shut on top of him...

James Morton (8)
Barley Fields Primary School, Ingleby Barwick

The Little Vampire

Once upon a time there lived a little boy called Tony. He was asleep. He heard a bang on his window. He peeped through the curtains and saw Rudolf the vampire. He asked Rudolf to come inside and play hide-and-seek. Tony's mum and dad were coming upstairs, so Rudolf had to hide behind the curtains. Tony's mum saw that he was asleep, so she closed the door. Out popped Rudolf from behind the curtains and he said, 'Boo! Your turn, Tony, to hide from me.'

Annabelle Staniford (8)

Barley Fields Primary School, Ingleby Barwick

Blind Tim

Once upon a time there lived a boy called Tim. He loved to go for walks in the forest but they kept on losing him. One day he fell down a hole and went forward in time to 2016. He saw lots of people looking at him because he smelt and was wearing animal skin. Later that day, he met some snakes called Sis and Hiss. They pushed him into an opticians and a black and white pair of glasses fell on his head. But because he didn't have any food, unfortunately he died.

Ava McSorley (8)
Barley Fields Primary School, Ingleby Barwick

Discovery Of Egypt

One day, a scientist called Ronald went to a pyramid in Egypt to find a mummy. He tried to look but there were two paths. He chose to go right. Following the path through the pyramid, he took a break and leaned against the wall. A tile moved and a door opened. Ronald found a hidden room. In the room was a coffin. He opened it and found a mummy. Ronald took a picture but it awoke the mummy and he ran away. Ronald felt frightened but he had a photo to show everyone.

Jakub Powlowski (8)
Barley Fields Primary School, Ingleby Barwick

The Mummy's Curse

The gold hunter was out searching for treasure when he saw a big pyramid. He thought there might be some treasure in there, some good treasure. When he went inside the pyramid, he found a big tomb. The curious hunter decided to open it. Out fell a coin and then a mummy. The hunter picked up the coin and started to run. The mummy chased him and in the end cornered him. He took back his coin and really hurt the hunter. This was called *the mummy's curse!*

Isobel Vaughan (8)
Barley Fields Primary School, Ingleby Barwick

Henry VIII's Jesters

Henry VIII's jester was woken by the clattering wind banging against the palace. The whole night was a stormy one with heavy rain. The jester went out to get food for the palace. It was really windy and all the trees were falling down by the stalls as the jester was walking by. Suddenly, a tree fell on top of him! Luckily, another jester was walking by and saw him. The other jester ran back to the palace and got Henry to lift the tree up. The jester was free!

Olivia Edwards (10)
Barley Fields Primary School, Ingleby Barwick

Into The Woods

In 501BC, the leaves started to fall and snow covered the ground. But soon, the ground started to shake. My claws shook in fear and my little heart pounded. I started to run as the monster chased me into the forest. Soon, I hurdled over twigs and pits as the monster chased me. A couple of minutes later, I found a pit. After I recovered, I walked out of the pit but it was dark and slimy. Something closed on me, then I realised I was dead meat. Or could I get away?

Katie Tuffnell (10)
Barley Fields Primary School, Ingleby Barwick

Usain Bolt

Usain Bolt is as fast as lightning. He is so fast he could be lightning. He started off decently fast, he got struck by lightning and that is what made him super fast. The wind howled as Bolt ran like lightning. Bolt heard a noise coming from the north. It sounded like creaking. He moved towards the noise and punched a monster in the face, then ran off fast. He came back but this time Bolt kicked the monster in the head. He came back and knocked the monster out.

Ashton Smith (9)
Barley Fields Primary School, Ingleby Barwick

The Queen Is Sentenced To Death!

The wind was howling through the streets of London. I was about to run away because I was going to be executed the next day. I jumped out of my bedroom window hoping I hadn't woken King Henry. I checked that King Henry wasn't following me. Oh no! King Henry was following with all his guards behind him. I was coming to the end of the street. He had caught me! The executioner was called. He took me to the block. His axe was sharpened. Then he did it...

Emily Garbutt (11)
Barley Fields Primary School, Ingleby Barwick

The Nervous Queen

I just woke up in Queen Victoria's bed. It was a bit of a squash and a squeeze. She seemed a little lost but then I think maybe cross. But she had just turned eighteen. It was only day one for her as our queen. She looked a little nervous but also keen, as today was her day to become my queen. I looked from her bed and nodded my head as she looked like a typical teen. I sat down beside her and whispered, 'I hope your reign is long and supreme.'

Grace Daniel (8)
Barley Fields Primary School, Ingleby Barwick

The Day I Met Muhammad Ali

The sun was shining in the jungle. They were face-to-face. Both refused to back down or give up. The champion was powerful but Ali was fast. Their gloves were raised. Punches were thrown, fists hitting faces and bodies. Just before the end of the eighth round, the challenger knocked out the champion. A brief silence, then the crowd erupted. I jumped to my feet, cheering my hero. Muhammad Ali had just won the greatest sporting event of the 20th century.

Kingsley McCarthy (8)
Barley Fields Primary School, Ingleby Barwick

Man On The Moon

I opened the door in a state of excitement. I stepped slowly into the atmosphere. Everywhere around me was dark, except for the shimmering stars. Something bright and shiny whizzed past me. I thought it was a flying saucer but then I realised it was a shooting star with an alien riding on it. I followed the alien. I tried to walk but I couldn't because there was no gravity so I had to jump and float. The alien took me to an... alien party!

Sarah Adamson (8)
Barley Fields Primary School, Ingleby Barwick

Who Am I?

I stepped out into the bright sunlight that seemed to blind me. The sound of the audience clapping, cheering and booing vibrated in my ears. The sand under my feet was soaked with blood and sweat. I felt nervous and curious about meeting my opponent. Was it animal or human? I took another step and raised my sword. My heart was pounding. I stopped and said to myself, '*I'm indestructible. I can do this. I'm a gladiator!*'

Alex Davison (10)
Barley Fields Primary School, Ingleby Barwick

The Bomb

The engine roared. The plane was shooting. The enemy was coming closer. The pilot held his breath before hurtling to the ground. Were they safe? German fighter planes soared across the sky. The tension was building as the German bomb thudded on the ground. *Pa doom!* was the sound the bomb made as it was only a few seconds away from blowing up another village. A brave British soldier dived to stop the bomb but it was too late...

Harriet Christie (10)

Barley Fields Primary School, Ingleby Barwick

The Mummy That Saved A Life

A long time ago in 1911BC, there was a girl who was poor. One day she was mining for gold. When she was digging, she found a room. It was dark and cold. She discovered a map which gave a clue to the next puzzle. She found a key to open a large wooden chest. In the chest was a mummy who looked dead but was alive. It opened its eyes and went, 'Boo!' The mummy helped her to get out of the cave. She finally arrived at the surface.

Caitlyn Stansfield (8)
Barley Fields Primary School, Ingleby Barwick

The Pharaoh's Bad Day

When he went into his newly built pyramid, he saw a mummy. He was running out of the pyramid when the door slammed shut and hit his face. When he woke up, he was on a table. Then the mummy said, 'One move and you will be turned into a mummy.' So when the mummy wasn't looking, he ran out of the room and got the mummy's coffin. He broke the door and ran out. He never went into a pyramid again and took off his crown.

Daniel Phillipson (8)
Barley Fields Primary School, Ingleby Barwick

Trapped In The Pyramid

Today, an important visitor came to Egypt and she didn't know there were pyramids there, so she decided to explore them. When she was in the pyramid, she saw there were booby traps and she fell in a hole. It was dark in the hole but luckily she had a torch. When she turned the torch on, she could see there were some ladders so she climbed them. She needed to get out of the pyramid, so she followed a path and it took her out.

Lana Thomson (9)
Barley Fields Primary School, Ingleby Barwick

A Mysterious Letter

Once, there lived a man called Stan Hollis. He was playing in his room when he heard the door knock. So he trotted downstairs and found a letter. He grabbed the letter and rushed upstairs, took it out of the envelope and read it. It was saying he had to go to the army. Stan felt scared but confident at the same time. He felt happy, excited, nervous and lucky. He put the letter down, lay on his bed and smiled. He was off to war.

Ethan Sawyer (8)
Barley Fields Primary School, Ingleby Barwick

The Pack Of Death

100 million years ago, the scary beasts came stalking the peaceful herd of Edmontosauruses. They were starving of course because of a 12-month drought. The leader charged and the hunt began! I watched from a safe distance as the beasts closed in on the Edmontosauruses. I couldn't believe how nimbly they attacked - again and again. I noticed they had claws that protruded from their first toe. It was a pack of... raptors.

Oliver Stonehouse (8)
Barley Fields Primary School, Ingleby Barwick

The Bombs Are Coming!

My heart skipped a beat! I knew it was coming, it was coming for me. The bombs were going to hit my village and wipe out the population. We had to get sheltered. I had to save everyone. After a few years, I joined the army so I could finally save my people and seek my revenge. Although I wasn't able to do everything I dreamt of (to save everyone). Just then, I had to protect a poor village. Then it happened...

Isabel Caddick (10)
Barley Fields Primary School, Ingleby Barwick

D-Day

The German rifles fired. Blood dripped from the air squadron's helmet. Engines spluttered as they soared through the sky. My mum was screaming at one of the German soldiers who had reached the top of the beaches and was stabbing my older brother to death. Brutal! Right? A French soldier came rushing through the old, wooden door but this German soldier was not going to give up without a fight to the death...

Zach Latcham (10)
Barley Fields Primary School, Ingleby Barwick

Bella And Her Dog's Dinosaur Adventure

Deep in the desert, where no one has been, sleeps a dinosaur. One day Bella and her dog approached the dinosaur's cave. They went inside and their eyes were shocked as they saw the dinosaur hugging a huge pile of gold and gems. They went over to the dinosaur. The dinosaur sniffed and woke up. Bella and her dog were in trouble. Would Bella and her dog escape? Read the next book to find out more...

Isabella Kathryn Walton (8)
Barley Fields Primary School, Ingleby Barwick

Jaws Of Death

As I opened the large, sturdy door, I heard a colossal roar that spread out all over the little city. My jaw dropped. My heart skipped a beat. The door smashed open and I was chased down the halls. I ran for my life. My heart pounded quicker than a torpedo. It came at me. I was cornered and that's when I saw a scaly figure with short hands and razor-sharp teeth. It was a dinosaur.

Jack Atkinson (10)
Barley Fields Primary School, Ingleby Barwick

The Bomb

I was playing in the school playground and saw a war plane. It took me a matter of seconds to realise it was the Germans. I said to my friend, 'That's the Germans.' A matter of seconds later, they stopped the plane. Then they dropped the bomb right near my friend. It killed him but I escaped. I had escaped with only a broken arm. I was really, really lucky.

Ryan Lynch (9)
Barley Fields Primary School, Ingleby Barwick

The Big Dinosaur Looks For Food And Leaves

The big dinosaur was hungry but he had nothing to eat. He was in the dry, dusty desert and wanted juicy leaves but there was nothing around him, except rocks and pebbles. He slowly walked up hills and in small valleys to find the juicy leaves. Eventually, he found the juicy leaves that he wanted but he was very tired of walking up the hills and through small valleys.

Poppy Tapster (7)
Barley Fields Primary School, Ingleby Barwick

The End Of The Egyptians

In 1640BC, a total of 46 pyramids were built and some people even thought William Shakespeare was going to be buried in one. But a few years later, some unexpected guests turned up, including King Tut and some aliens. But the aliens started to blow things up and in that process, King Tut disappeared and was never seen again.

Sam Parry (9)
Barley Fields Primary School, Ingleby Barwick

The Mysterious Shadow

All was quiet until we heard a crack! Then we carried on but Daisy got caught and told me and Emily to run, but then Emily got caught. I ran for my life until I tripped over a tree root. When I slowly got up and got my breath back, I looked up and saw a shadow. It came closer and closer. It was a...

Lilia Long (8)
Barley Fields Primary School, Ingleby Barwick

The Plague Is Spreading

In the heart of London, the gruesome killing disease was spreading quicker every day. From house to house, sooner or later I would catch it. Oh no, I began to get massive lumps the size of oranges, and an endless cough. There was an 'X' on my door. I had caught the plague...

Beth Ward (9)

Barley Fields Primary School, Ingleby Barwick

The Deadly Air Raids

I awakened to a hammering siren and immediately darted to the shelter.

Whilst in darkness, I heard an ear-piercing *bang!*

Clattering out of the shelter, my eyes locked shut and my fingers crossed; I prayed it wasn't my home...

I anxiously unlocked my eyes; my heart stopped. Rubble.

No mum, dad or home... just me. *Jake.*

As I began to look around, a glimmer of hope emerged as Josh came to see if I was OK. He said me and Jake would have to come and live with him. Then I was evacuated to my auntie's... still memorising home - rubble.

Oliver Elsdon-Whitfield (10)
Great Smeaton Academy Primary School, Northallerton

The Battle In The Sea

Scanning the vast ocean, our captain spotted the smoking wreck of an English boat that had been bombed - we were there to save them.
The Germans were expecting us...
Explosive canisters rained down on us; water aggressively came cascading in, flooding the cabin. Desperately, we tried everything we'd learnt to get the submarine to the glimmering surface.
Retaliating against the attack, we sent several steaming torpedoes up at the German boat above, successfully sinking the frustrated enemy. It came crashing down on top of us. *Crash! Clank!*
'Mayday! Mayday!'
The terrified crew and their battered boats were never seen again...

George Gayer (10)
Great Smeaton Academy Primary School, Northallerton

The Dog Hero

'Goodbye,' the RAF called; Edgar was beginning to set off to the dogfight.

Booom!

'I've been hit!' he screamed into the radio. The fire roared like a tiger growling at its prey. The wings snapped off and the propeller flew away as the plane smashed into the field. 'Help!' His leg hurt and turned bright purple.

Suddenly, he heard a noise. Quickly, the noise faded and was replaced with a siren. They carried him into the ambulance.

'That dog led us to you,' said a voice.

Looking at the dog, he realised it was his own. He'd saved him.

Fran Marshall (9)
Great Smeaton Academy Primary School, Northallerton

The Sacrifice

Emily's husband was at war. The children she loved had been evacuated to the beautiful countryside. Her family - gone.

A letter arrived.

Was John dead? No, she'd been asked to create clothes for women.

Emily created lots of women's garments as the letter requested. The praise that was given was amazing. One woman, who was wealthy, said she wanted a picturesque dress of lace.

Tapping her foot she said, 'Make it and a reward shall await.' The only lace she had was her wedding dress.

Daringly, Emily sat down at her sewing machine with her dress and began to sew.

Bethany Brown (11)

Great Smeaton Academy Primary School, Northallerton

Hidden

After endless hours of ruthlessly raiding houses searching for Jews, the emotionless monsters had finally gone.

Hidden away in a secret space - cleverly disguised by a painting - we decided it was safe to come out at last. Devastation surrounded us; our belongings were strewn around the room.

'They're back!' my brother shrieked as he witnessed a truck pulling up for the second time. Flooded with fear, we darted back to our hiding place, anxiously waiting in silence whilst the soldiers raided our home. Again. Would they find us this time?

'Shh! What's that?' questioned the chief soldier. 'Move that painting!'

Maegan Sharp (11)
Great Smeaton Academy Primary School, Northallerton

Secret Spies

Operation Jaws, a mission to secretly spy on the German artillery, was about to commence.

Flying together for the first time, three pilots swooped over the channel in the early hours of the morning. The cascading rain created a waterfall on the steamed-up windows; the pilots remained focussed - their faces unreadable.

Drifting down, the plane landed perfectly on French soil. A wooden sign was uncovered by one of the spies; he unsheathed his faithful knife and, with steady hands, cautiously removed the plastic cover. 'Un mile à l'Allemagne' - one mile to Germany.

The three spies were heading into enemy territory...

Casey Chapman (11)
Great Smeaton Academy Primary School, Northallerton

The Magic Adventure

The trees blew as they walked into the dark, gloomy museum. They were greeted by Cleopatra, which was a bit off. As they walked into the dark, creepy room, a mummy came out of nowhere. Eva, Tilly and Ellie sprinted for their lives. Suddenly, they all fell off a cliff. Down and down they went until *bang!* There they were in Egypt. Eva shouted as loud as she could, 'Look, there's the lion statue with a man's head!' They all rushed ahead. Then they saw a pyramid. Inside were lots of paintings. Cleopatra appeared and turned them into mummies!

Kacey-Leigh Brunton (9)
Green Gates Primary School, Redcar

A Holiday To Egypt

A holiday to Egypt was going to be great and exciting for Kacey, Courtney and myself. We went to visit the pyramids. Inside they had all the paintings and writing from ancient times which was out of this world. Then they heard creepy noises and eyes were staring at them from everywhere. It was scary. Then a tomb opened. Inside was a mummy. They got very scared and ran outside to find someone had been messing about with things in the pyramids and it was not a real mummy. It was scary but they can laugh about it now.

Jasmyne Walker (9)
Green Gates Primary School, Redcar

Ruby And Warren's Magical Trip

Once upon a time there lived a brother and sister called Ruby and Warren. One day, both of them went in the attic and they saw a huge cupboard but it was locked. Luckily, Ruby had a hair clip to unlock the chain. As Ruby opened it, they were disappointed because there was only an ordinary clock. While Ruby was thinking, Warren put his hand through it and went to Egypt. So did Ruby. When they were walking, Warren met Cleopatra. She was amazed to see her. But was there a safe way home?

Ruby Campbell (9)
Green Gates Primary School, Redcar

Blood Feud

'Poseidon!' I yelled. The sky turned quiet. All the gods came gathering round to watch a good fight between brothers. 'How could you do this to me, your own brother? Come and fight me.'

As Poseidon rose from the water, he looked angry, as if he was about to burst. 'What do you want, brother?' he raged.

A rumble went through the crowd. This would be a good fight. In the blink of an eye, a whole army of sea creatures appeared next to him. I started to back away because I didn't have an army of my own...

Isobel Coe (9)
Kader Academy, Middlesbrough

What's Happening?

Bang! Tiles were falling off the roof, pots were smashing! Could this be the end of Pompeii? I ran down the stairs and sped out of the door. Augusta dashed out as soon as I did and then Marilla appeared. 'Let's go to the harbour!' she screamed. We ran, not knowing where to go but we could see men loading crates into boats, so we assumed that was the harbour. Rocks were flying into my face and almost every building was burnt down. When we got there, I got into the last boat, but my friends couldn't reach. What now?

Lucy Richardson (9)
Kader Academy, Middlesbrough

Florence Nightingale

Once upon a time there was a naughty little girl called Florence. When she was fully grown up, she became a nurse, not one that cared for people but one that killed people!

During the war which her father started, she was the nurse in charge. As she was in charge, she could get away with killing people. She hypnotised other nurses to do it as well. Her evil plan was to kill everyone except her and her father. After a long war with lots of deaths, her evil plan had worked!

Evelyn Woodward (8)
Kader Academy, Middlesbrough

We've Got You Now!

Guns were shot, the wind blustered through the cold, snowy air, men drowned in the thick white blanket that laid under their feet. Would this war never end? As a speeding bullet zipped right past me, I ran for my life and I landed safely in front of my block of angry men. They were shooting and fighting the defensive French. But just as we thought we had been victorious the leader, Napoleon Bonaparte, ordered an enormous cannon! The men were terrified! I had thought of a spectacular idea! I ran to the cannon and clogged it with the butt of my gun! They saw me and surrounded me! I couldn't escape...

Alexander Hasler (9)
Kader Academy, Middlesbrough

If Mount Vesuvius Was An Ice Cream

There stood a sundae full of blistering and smooth toffee sauce, covered with whipped cream and canned fruit. Smartie people lived in nearby gingerbread houses and they watched from afar, unaware the great sundae was rumbling. Suddenly, the ground started to shake and crack. The air filled with the sticky smell of marshmallows and the sound of popping candy was deafening. Hundreds and thousands exploded from the sundae, causing the toffee sauce to escape towards the houses. Smartie people were covered with deadly, chewy marshmallows and got stuck where they stood forever and ever.

Harry Bell (9)
Kader Academy, Middlesbrough

The Blood Sucker!

I heard the most horrifying sound. Terrified, anxious, petrified, I stepped inside the cold, dark room. There were thousand-year-old books that hadn't been read for years. The ceiling was drowned in blood and a wind-up box played haunting music. I saw a silhouette walking towards me. I blinked twice and it disappeared. I peered inside the cupboard, nothing there. I turned around. Something bit me on my neck and started sucking my blood. Every ounce of blood it took, I was getting weaker. But now my ghost roams around searching for help that cannot be found.

Zahra Rashad (8)
Kader Academy, Middlesbrough

The Execution Of Anne Boleyn!

The start of this ominous day was terrible. People started screaming and shouting as Anne Boleyn was executed with blood oozing all down her clothes. I heard Henry VIII shout as loud as he could. I was there, watching Anne Boleyn getting executed. It was the worst day of my life. Suddenly, I heard a strange tip-tapping noise. I looked to my left, no one was there. Then I looked to my right. That was the same, no one was there. I looked behind me. There was a man in a black robber's costume who came towards me with an axe...

Iqra Ali (9)
Kader Academy, Middlesbrough

The Beast...

The wind howled like a wolf being attacked on a starless night. Petrified, the hairs on my neck stood on end. I heard a roar! Although I wanted to run, my legs stayed rooted to the spot. Suddenly, out of the dark, misty wood, a menacing dinosaur trudged out. Diving into an old log, I waited, keeping eye contact with the beast. It let out a blood-curdling *roar!* I jumped. Without warning, the log started to roll! I leapt out and landed in a patch of mud. Muddy and cold, I came face-to-face with a dinosaur...

Alisha Hussain (10)
Kader Academy, Middlesbrough

Her

House doors slammed and curtains twitched. I felt eyes were staring intently at me. I started to get quite scared; there was a really bad pong that hung around the street. I kept walking and soon I was there, I was at the graveyard. I opened the unpainted gate. It screeched and I hesitated. Then I crept in and edged towards his grave. I bent once to put flowers down, then I saw a dark shadow leaning over me. I froze with fear. Isolated, I turned my head to see a knife in his hand! I gasped. He struck fiercely...

Naiomi Pye (11)
Kader Academy, Middlesbrough

The Sarcophagus

It all happened in ancient Egypt. It was a long time ago and some people heard a scream! The sun blazed and burned the skin of people and made them turn red. As the sarcophagus burned the last traitor, it looked like stone. Yes, the last person had been turned to stone. Every time he turned someone into stone, he needed a rest and the sarcophagus decided to do that. Oh, how he loved turning people into stone or making people burn to death. So as he tried it, he turned red. He boiled and that is the tale.

Skye Chen (8)
Kader Academy, Middlesbrough

Blood, Death And A New Wife

As she lay frozen like a statue in her bed, she heard a banging sound on the door, then footsteps. After that, her door creaked open. It was a bloodthirsty executor ready to kill her! She went outside with her hands shaking. At last she knelt down and put her head on the piece of wood that lay before her. Outside she was strong, but inside she felt like running away. The crowds cheered as the axe rose and, with one fatal swoop, Anne's head dropped to the ground. Who would be Henry's wife now?

Biba Lairini-Taylor (10)
Kader Academy, Middlesbrough

Untitled

The sound of the cold air behind my ears and the thought of getting attacked scared me. I walked through the ice-cold surroundings, thinking about what could happen to me. Then I saw a tall, white shadow chasing me from a distance. My heart stopped. I didn't breathe. I just ran and ran. The shadow chased me until I turned to see a polar bear with knife-shaped teeth and life-threatening claws. My life was at its end. The fierce polar bear reached down to grab me. I could do nothing but scream...

Scarlett Armstrong (10)
Kader Academy, Middlesbrough

The Beast!

The wind howled like a wolf under the sombre midnight sky. The trees swayed ferociously, scared of what was to come. My legs ran as fast as they could carry me. I couldn't believe it. My mind was blown. There came the beast with hunger in his eyes and death in his claws. His eyes were as red as blood, fresh from a body. His claws were as sharp as a knife used by a murderer. *Grrrr!* The beast bellowed. Within the blink of an eye, it was face-to-face with me. It was... Beowulf!

Brandon Pollock (10)
Kader Academy, Middlesbrough

Disasters To Happy Endings

Every step I took, it just felt like they were getting closer. I couldn't handle it. I didn't know what it was, everything just felt a blur. I could barely run. I suddenly started to slow down. The big, scary monster was so close! I thought it was the end of me, until a big, muscular man came across on a vine and grabbed me. We flew away in the moonlight and landed on a tree. He kept making noises. I couldn't understand him, but I could tell he was saying I was safe.

Heidi Elizabeth Peat (9)
Kader Academy, Middlesbrough

The Day Things Changed

It was a good day in Pompeii. Birds were singing and flowers were blooming, up until a tremor hit us. Bricks were falling and looking into the distance, I saw Mount Vesuvius erupting. Smoke was billowing out of a once beautiful mountain, but in the streets, parents were gathering up their children as ash rained down on the buildings behind. I suddenly realised that it was raining on me, so I needed to run. Tripping up, I fell to the ground, hoping the gods would save me...

Kai Hodge (9)
Kader Academy, Middlesbrough

The Curse Of Cleopatra's Army

It was coming. As sand whipped around, it got closer. As the wind pushed me back, it got nearer. There was nowhere to hide. It and its army were getting quicker and quicker, closer and closer by the second. I wanted to run but I stayed rooted to the spot. Then silence glided through the air. Everything was still. Nobody moved a muscle. What was going on? 'Charge!' Cleopatra's army. I should never have gone near that pyramid...

Elizabeth Morrissey (10)
Kader Academy, Middlesbrough

Dinosaur Chase

The wind howled and trees stalked upon the shadows. I walked slowly but looked back and there stood the monster before me! It was a dinosaur! My heart thumped. I squeezed my body as tight as I could and shivered. I only knew one thing and that was to run. I ran as fast as my legs could carry me but the dinosaur was getting closer and closer. I hid behind a cliff until the dinosaur left. What would happen next? Do you know?

Goodness Onuh (8)
Kader Academy, Middlesbrough

Altering The Past

Once, there was a girl called Violet who always dreamed of going back in time. One day in particular she found a feather. Whenever she touched the feather, heat spread through her fingers. Then she got whisked up into the air and dumped in a village where all the people were wearing what looked like tunics. 'I can't believe this!' Violet said.

'Can't believe what?' exclaimed a Roman soldier.

'I... I don't know,' Violet said, rather frightened.

'Huh? Well scram, little girl!'

She felt a slight tingle again. Without realising what was happening, she was back home.

Hannah Armstrong (8)
Levendale Primary School, Yarm

Chariot Tunnel

Sam and I were at our favourite park with the old stone walls and tunnels. Diving into a tunnel, to my amazement there was a man dressed in a white sheet. 'Hurry, your chariot awaits!' he said. Feeling scared, I followed. Hooves were pounding, dust flying and crowds roaring. My heart beat so fast I couldn't breathe.

I felt someone ruffling my hair. Turning to see, it was Sam. 'Are you OK?' he said.

Looking around, I was now staring up at the underside of the tunnel. There were sketches and strange writing. Was this a warning not to enter?

William Carr (8)
Levendale Primary School, Yarm

The Battle

Maximus could feel his heart beating faster than he had ever felt it before. Stood alongside the other soldiers in his legion, this felt so different from how he remembered during training. Maximus had always dreamed of being a Roman soldier. He was strong, tall, as well as being loyal, courageous and disciplined. Maximus' first battle as a Roman soldier was seconds away from starting. Now stood in battle formation, drenched in sweat, his cheeks bulged as he held his breath. Dagger in one hand, shield in the other, Maximus waited for his centurion to give the order. 'Charge!'

Max Norman (8)
Levendale Primary School, Yarm

Ben's Naughty Joke

Alex the Roman was walking down a cold, dark, cobbled road when he heard a noise, *woooo!* Alex turned around, shaking and scared. *Woooo!* He heard it again. He turned around again to find an Egyptian mummy. Alex screamed, 'Argh!' The mummy ran but Alex grabbed and held on tight to its bandages until there were no bandages left. The mummy stopped only to reveal it was not a mummy but Alex's friend, Ben who was just playing a joke. Naughty Ben! Ben laughed and so did Alex as they walked back up the cold, dark, cobbled path together.

Ellis Leason (8)
Levendale Primary School, Yarm

Joe The Champion Cyclist

Once, there was a boy called Joe. He lived in River Town. His mum wanted him to be a tennis champion but Joe had other thoughts. He wanted to be a cycling champion. Every time he went to his tennis lessons, he sneaked off to the cycle track instead. Soon, his mum found out what he had been doing and she was mad! She grounded Joe. Naughty Joe carefully sneaked out of the house and went to a cycling race. He actually won! When the newspaper came, his mum looked at the front page and saw Joe! She decided to let him follow his dream.

Oliver Kibble (8)
Levendale Primary School, Yarm

The Mummy's Coming

Long legs and pointy feet were following me. I was dodging the pyramids and panting for breath. 'Help!' I yelled but no one heard. My pigtails flew behind me. I had to stop so I leant on a nearby pyramid. The mummy was getting closer by the second. But when I came face-to-face with the mummy, I was forced not to look directly into the mummy's gleaming red eyes. I was going to run when I grabbed hold of one of the mummy's loose bandages and pulled. It went spinning around and around. The mummy was now dead.

Holly De Main (8)
Levendale Primary School, Yarm

The Final Journey

I was working as a cabin girl on Captain Cook's ship, The Endeavour. The sky was dark. The waves were crashing into the ship and the only light I could see was the lightning flashing above our heads. The storm lasted for ages. I woke, the sea was calm, I heard a voice calling, 'Land ahoy!' Through the mist I could see land. We arrived on the island. The local people tried to steal our boats. Captain Cook kidnapped their chief as revenge. In the attempt, a fight broke out and Captain Cook was killed by natives.

Ruby Walton (8)
Levendale Primary School, Yarm

The Princess In A Bag

Once upon a time there was a princess who didn't like dragons. She didn't like dragons because one day her window was open and a dragon flew past. The dragon flew by and fired some fire in the princess's window. The princess was so sad, she ran away to the beach. On the beach there was a little cave that led to a man singing. She walked into the cave and saw a Viking. The Viking was making fish stew. She said hello and the Viking turned around. The princess told the Viking all about the dragon.

Amelie Rose Kibble (8)
Levendale Primary School, Yarm

Battle Time

The wind whistled. The Britons were back, coming for revenge. I was so scared. This could be the first but last battle I was ever going to have. I took my shield and sword and got into place with the other soldiers. My heart was beating like a bass drum. Would we win or would we lose? I was scared but excited. I had been training for this moment for months. The Britons looked fierce but that wasn't going to make me scared. The Romans were in it to win it. I clenched my fists. This was the big moment.

Lucy Makepeace (8)
Levendale Primary School, Yarm

Egyptian Magic

I was sitting beside the River Nile. My servants were feeding me grapes and red wine. It was a very warm evening. Suddenly, I heard a loud roar. My servants dropped everything and ran. I looked up and standing over me was a ferocious sphinx. I looked around and could see that he had escaped from a tomb. I saw a small glass bottle lying on the ground. One of the servants must have dropped it. I quickly grabbed the bottle and threw the potion at the sphinx. He magically disappeared!

Lois Hudson-Foster (8)
Levendale Primary School, Yarm

Mummy's After Me

On a hot, dusty night inside the pyramid, I was looking for gold. I crept along the tunnel with only a candle's light to guide my way. As I walked down the dark, creepy tunnel, I felt like someone had been watching me. Suddenly, two beady eyes opened in front of me. I dropped the candle and sprinted out of there as fast as my legs would go. It was a mummy...

Grace Forster (8)
Levendale Primary School, Yarm

The Magic Cave

Once upon a time, a girl called Lilly went into a cave and she was in Roman times. She did not know any of these people because she was in Roman times. Lilly became a Roman soldier even though she was a girl. She went on a mission to kill Celts. All the Celts died except for Boudicca who was hidden in the trees. Lilly went back home.

Abi Edwards (7)
Levendale Primary School, Yarm

The Poor Ninja

A man named Mr Dooley was a poor man. One day he found loads of rocks and made a sword. He went out to get some food so he didn't finish it. He came back and finished his sword and he decorated it as well. He put his favourite design on it, then he went to his comfortable bed.
The next day, Mr Dooley got his sword and went out hunting. He came back and left his sword. He went out again and found a stranger. The stranger had a sword but he killed the stranger.

Emily Leaver (8)
Silver Tree Primary School, Durham

Minotaur At War

There it it! Sparta and Athens at war. Blood squirts all over the ground and I hear everyone scream. 'Yay! Spartans are the champions.' I hear loud stamping until I see the Minotaur jump off a building. The Minotaur starts killing some Spartans. Oh no! I start seeing blood everywhere again. Now I'm running for my life because the Minotaur is chasing after me. I see a bow and arrow as I'm running, so I pick it up and shoot the Minotaur. It isn't enough to kill him, so I shoot it again. Now he's dead. Now in Heaven.

Harvey Johnson (8)
Silver Tree Primary School, Durham

Stone Age Fight

One day, the Stone Age people were doing their normal things in their camp. Then, all of a sudden, 100 soldiers came and fought the Stone Age soldiers. The fight went on for hours. There were dead bodies everywhere! After every soldier was killed, it was just the two kings. The two kings started fighting. It was very tough but there was one dead king and one king alive. The alive king was the Stone Age people's king. The handsome king was called Mr Martin. He was the best king in the world.

Charlie Martin (8)
Silver Tree Primary School, Durham

The Heap Is Coming!

A man called Du knew a heap of mammoths were coming that day. He made axes, spears and fire. A mammoth looked at him and Du went and attacked it. All the mammoths were watching. They were mad! Du was eating it. It made the mammoths madder. They charged at Du but Du got a giant stone and blocked the cave entrance. The mammoths charged. *Boom! Boom!* But they still didn't get in. Then the mammoths broke through but just wanted a cuddle. Then a saber-toothed tiger came and ate Du.

Jack Wilson (8)
Silver Tree Primary School, Durham

Peat Bog Time

Lof went and chopped trees. Lof is a caveman. After chopping trees, he met a dog called Sparky. Then Sparky and Lof went on with their walk. Soon, they came to a herd of buffalo. He could also see elephants. Lof had a cunning plan. He'd jump on the buffalo's back and when he got to the elephant's herd, slice his axe at them. He'd bring dinner back. After eating, Lof and Sparky walked a little bit more. Suddenly, *splash!* Lof fell to his death in a peat bog! Oh no!

Ellie Snowdon (8)
Silver Tree Primary School, Durham

Minotaur Attacks

One day I went to the Olympics and watched the race. The runner that came first was really fast and he came up to me and said, 'Thanks for the cheering.' I saw something out of the corner of my eye. It had two horns and a bull's head, legs and feet. It held an axe which was very sharp and the creature sprinted fiercely at the man who won the race, so I warned him but he didn't hear me. Out of the corner of his eye, he saw the Minotaur, so he sprinted away quickly.

Bailey Martyn (8)
Silver Tree Primary School, Durham

The Adventure

A long time ago, there was an adventurer called Jack and he really liked to travel to different shaped islands and places. One time he went to a small forest on a new island. His partner, Ben, who he stayed with most of the time was also a great memoriser. Suddenly, they got attacked by a big, ferocious beast, so Ben memorised the deadly animal because they might not remember this moment. After that they returned home so they could be safe and sound. Ben showed Jack the artwork.

Ryan Cleminson (8)
Silver Tree Primary School, Durham

The Machine Is Coming

One day in Sparta there was an inventor called Lucky. He spent months on this thing called the machine. One day it was completed, so he turned it on and shouted, 'It's alive!' Then it was destroying the city! So he went into his lair and met a hero who wasn't actually a hero, he was an inventor too, so they thought of a plan. Lucky could distract it and Hero could cut all the wires, so they tried it and it worked. The village used the pieces of it to make a sign.

Lucy Sugden (8)
Silver Tree Primary School, Durham

Dead Or Alive?

A long time ago in 0AD in a small village, there lived a man called Cooner. One day, Cooner was wandering outside of the village and saw a cave. It was dark and damp. He slowly walked towards the cave. Then he went inside. Cooner walked until he saw a tomb and a torch. Cooner picked up the torch and stared at the tomb. Carefully, he opened the tomb up. Inside was a dead king. Cooner slowly bent down and picked up the torch but when he stood up, the king's eyes were open...

Ellie Ayre (7)
Silver Tree Primary School, Durham

Hunting For Animals

In the past, some Stone Age people were very hungry. They showed they were hungry by actions. Because they were waiting for their father, they couldn't go hunting. They were so hungry that they were going to starve. Finally, the father was back. They all asked what he'd done. He said, 'I've been chopping wood and making an axe out of that.' Now finally they could go hunting for their food. They were so good at hunting, they should be masters at it.

Tyler Rennie (8)
Silver Tree Primary School, Durham

Skylar The Ship Saver [Well...]

'This chicken's lovely,' boasted Mum.

'The turkey's better,' interrupted Dad.

Crash! The whole dinner party dashed towards the window.

'Argh!' shrieked Chrissy in horror. 'Get out!'

Within a blink of an eye, we were all in the sea. There's only room for one hero on this ship... and it was going to be me! When our lifeboat hit the water, I swiftly dived out of the boat and started to swim towards the front of the ship. As the boat started to tip, everything, including the chef's giant Yorkshire pudding, fell out. I managed to plug the hole with it.

Isabel Dobson (11)

St Margaret Clitherow's Catholic Primary School, Middlesbrough

Defend Rome!

The barbarians didn't and wouldn't stop pushing. The line was trembling before the barbarians. 'Stay strong, men!' screamed the general. Caesar froze in horror as the terrifying barbarians breached the wall. Caesar had to do something quickly. He ran up one of Rome's towers and gathered some arrows and a bow. He raised his bow and aimed at the barbarian king. He felt a power to destroy the barbarians. He let go of the arrow screaming. The arrow duplicated into 500,000 arrows. The barbarians were slaughtered and Caesar became the new emperor of Rome.

Christopher Brown (11)
St Margaret Clitherow's Catholic Primary School, Middlesbrough

Darkness

'Boo!' The crowds jeered as she stepped towards the vicious, merciless swordsman who would soon end her life. Anne Boleyn, her heart pounding, touched her neck for what would be the last time. Looking at the people who had come to see her doom, she saw terrified people, people bellowing insults and the king sitting with his new wife. She took a deep breath, then rested her pale neck on the wood. With terror in his heart, the executioner put his sword high into the air. Anne closed her eyes and bit her lip nervously. In three, two, one... darkness.

Isabel Willet (11)
St Margaret Clitherow's Catholic Primary School, Middlesbrough

Titanic

Crash! The enormous boat smashed into the bitter iceberg. All of a sudden, Rose and Jack were terrified. While Jack was tied up to a pole in a flooded locker room, Rose was energetically and desperately trying to free him in a rush. A few moments later he was free and running through the freezing water with Rose, trying to get on the deck. Minutes passed. Boats were full and some were broken. Struggling to survive, Jack was shivering out of his skin and suddenly, he died. Rose was rescued but was sadly crying because she missed Jack.

Leigh Davey (11)
St Margaret Clitherow's Catholic Primary School, Middlesbrough

The Psychotic Leader

As the wind howled, the whimper of a wolf echoed through the empty streets. While the hunter was hunting, the king was wrecking his palace. One of his men snuck out and met up with the hunter to ask him to kill the king because he was a psychopath, destroying everything. As the hunter drew closer, he got an arrow ready. Sneakily climbing to his balcony, he knew if he missed he'd be dead. He took the shot, killing the king. After the king was dead, he disposed of the body by burning. The only memory is his crown.

Ben Wright (11)
St Margaret Clitherow's Catholic Primary School, Middlesbrough

Ancient Egypt

The huge, sandy pyramid came tumbling down with a thud. Me and Sienna ran as fast as we could away, before we got crushed. All of a sudden, we saw a light. As we got closer, it got bigger and bigger. It led to a room which was empty. Suddenly, the door slammed shut. We were locked in. Walking around slowly in the dark, I tripped over. There was a rope tied against two walls and it was a booby trap. Turning around quickly to see what was behind me, we heard a banging noise. It was Tutankhamun...

Annie Williams (11)
St Margaret Clitherow's Catholic Primary School, Middlesbrough

Years of YoungWriters

YOUNG WRITERS INFORMATION

We hope you have enjoyed reading this book – and that you will continue to in the coming years.

If you're a young writer who enjoys reading and creative writing, or the parent of an enthusiastic poet or story writer, do visit our website www.youngwriters.co.uk. Here you will find free competitions, workshops and games, as well as recommended reads, a poetry glossary and our blog.

If you would like to order further copies of this book, or any of our other titles give us a call or visit **www.youngwriters.co.uk**.

Young Writers
Remus House
Coltsfoot Drive
Peterborough
PE2 9BF

(01733) 890066
info@youngwriters.co.uk

'HE CAME, HE SAW, HE CONKED US'!